DISNEY'S

THE LITTLE MERMAID

GREEN-EYED PEARL

by Suzanne Weyn

illustrations by Fred Marvin

DISNEY PRESS

NEW YORK

For Carolan Suzanne Weyn,
a swimmer, sunner, seashore sweetie.
A little mermaid.

Produced by arrangement with Chardiet Unlimited, Inc.

Library of Congress Catalog Card Number: 92-53938

ISBN: 1-56282-250-0

FIRST EDITION

1 3 5 7 9 10 8 6 4 2

DISNEY's
THE LITTLE MERMAID

GREEN-EYED PEARL

Merpeople from all across the ocean were filling the seats of King Triton's Great Concert Hall. The annual Independence Day celebration was about to begin. The musicians gathered together on the stage while Sebastian the crab checked over his list. As royal conductor, it was his job to make sure the concert ran smoothly.

"Are all the performers here?" he asked.

"I'm here, Sebastian, sweetie!" said Bubbles the blowfish. She straightened her tall sea-fruit hat. "I'm ready to sing, sing, sing!"

"I'm here, too," said the Duke of Sole, flipping his seaweed cape behind him. "And I'm ready to boogie down."

Sebastian checked the performers' names off his list one by one. Then he turned to the princesses. "Are you girls ready to sing?" Sebastian asked. King Triton's seven daughters were well known for their beautiful voices.

"Oh, yes," said Aquata, the oldest. She spoke quickly. "Quite ready. Perfectly ready. No problem at all."

Sebastian looked at Aquata. "Something must be wrong," he muttered to himself. "That girl is too jittery. I wonder what the trouble is."

All at once Sebastian knew. It's the same trouble that's always the trouble! he thought.

"All right," he demanded. "Where is she?"

"Where is who?" asked Andrina sweetly.

Just then a pretty, petite mermaid zoomed through the front entrance of the concert hall, her thick red hair flowing behind her.

"Hi!" Ariel greeted them all with a bright smile. "I'm not late, am I? Well, I know I'm a little late. Sorry. But I did get here before the concert started, didn't I?"

Sebastian rolled his eyes. "Just start working on your scales, girls."

"Why? What's wrong with my scales?" gasped Adella, looking down at her tail. "I polished my scales this morning. Right after curling my hair and filing my nails. I think my scales look quite shiny. I don't see why I have to work on—"

"He means *musical* scales," Alana told her.

"Oh," said Adella. She smiled at Sebastian. "Never mind."

"These girls will be the death of me," Sebastian mumbled.

The moment Sebastian was gone, the sisters crowded around Ariel. "Thank goodness you made it," Attina told her. "Sebastian was about to burst his shell."

"I, for one, am getting tired of covering for you all the time," said Arista.

"I'm sorry," said Ariel. "I was out swimming and I lost track of the time."

"You're always losing track of the time!" sighed Aquata. "Just what do you do on those swims, anyway?"

Ariel shrugged. "This and that." She wanted to tell her sisters about her adventures, but she couldn't take the chance. If her father ever found out what she was up to, he wouldn't like it. Not one bit.

King Triton had decreed that it was strictly forbidden to explore sunken ships. But that was precisely Ariel's most favorite thing to do! She was so curious about the humans who lived on the land up above that she wanted to know everything about them. So she spent hours swimming among the wrecked ships at the bottom of the sea, collecting various treasures and hiding them in a secret grotto she had discovered not too far from the palace. Nobody knew about the grotto except for her best friend, Flounder. And he was sworn to secrecy!

"The important thing is that you're here now," said Alana. All the sisters nodded their agreement and went to look at the crowd.

"I've never seen such a huge audience," Arista said.

"Oh, look," said Adella, coming alongside Arista. "There's that awful Countess Oystera. She's trying to cram herself into that little seat next to Father."

Ariel watched as the plump merwoman gathered her long dress over one of her fat, flabby arms and squeezed her very large body into the very small seat. What a sight! Ariel thought, giggling to herself. Oystera finally settled down into the chair, smiled at King Triton, and let out a huge sigh of relief.

"She tells everyone that the king is her dear, dear friend," said Attina.

"But Father doesn't really like her, does he?" asked Alana.

"Of course not," Aquata said. "Father is just being polite." She wrinkled her nose. "Look who's with her—that dreadful little sneak, Pearl!"

Seated beside the portly countess was her daughter, Pearl, who every few minutes primped her long blond hair to make sure it looked perfect.

"That girl is so vain," said Adella, smoothing the waves of her own dark hair.

The sisters giggled.

"What?" asked Adella. "What's so funny?"

"You're right, Adella," Andrina snickered. "She's the one person in all the ocean who's vainer than you are."

"Ohhh, take that back," Adella cried angrily. Andrina laughed and spun away with Adella chasing after her.

"That Pearl has all the adults fooled," said Attina. "They think she's so sweet."

At that moment Sebastian rapped his stand with his conductor's baton. The show was about to begin. The sisters took their places in the wings and watched as the Duke of Sole belted out his first number.

The princesses were the last to perform. For their first song, each sister held the next one's tail. They swam in a circle as they sang about a silly fish who wouldn't let go of his own tail. The audience broke into gales of laughter. King Triton laughed harder and louder than anyone. He was so proud of his daughters.

For their last song, the mermaids sang about the beauties of the ocean. Near the end of the piece Ariel had a solo. "The starfish swim in the night waters," she sang in her clear, sweet voice. "Ahhhh-ahhh-ahhhh. Ahhhh-ahhh-ahhhhhh!"

When the music stopped, the audience

burst into loud applause. "Bravo!" someone in the crowd cheered.

The sisters all came forward and bowed. Ariel looked over at her father. His white beard floated in front of him; he looked very proud.

As Ariel swam off the stage toward her father, she saw he was talking to Countess Oystera.

"Pearl could stay with *us*," Ariel heard her father say.

"What a gracious offer!" the Countess exclaimed. "The Count and I have been longing to take this vacation for ages. But, as I said, Pearl simply refuses to come. She just hates traveling. If she could stay here, it would solve the problem! Thank you, dear, dear King Triton!"

"Ariel and Pearl are the same age. I'm sure they'll have fun together," the King said.

Ariel's heart skipped a beat. Spending time with Pearl was about the most unpleasant thing she could think of. Pearl was the most conceited, most selfish, nastiest merperson Ariel had ever met!

Pearl smiled up at Triton. "I would simply

adore staying at the palace," she said, batting her big green eyes at him. "It was so grand of you to ask!"

Ariel swam after her father as he returned to the palace.

"Father, please don't let Pearl stay here," she begged. "She'll make my life miserable. You don't know her."

"Ariel, I can't go back on my offer," King Triton said. Together they swam through the front door. The merguards bowed silently as the two passed.

"I know!" said Ariel. "You could send a messenger to Countess Oystera. Tell her I've come down with a case of sea pox. Horrible spots all over my face, and it's contagious. Pearl won't want to stay then. Please. Oh, please!"

King Triton sighed. "Ariel, I'm sorry, but what's done is done. Besides, Pearl seems like a lovely girl to me. We'll not discuss this any further."

Ariel could tell from the look on her father's face that he meant it. And so it was that several days later Ariel stood and watched Pearl's arrival at the palace.

"Announcing the Countessa Pearl," a royal sea horse messenger called.

Ariel sighed as Pearl made her grand entrance into the hallway. A parade of large snails crawled in behind her, carrying her many suitcases on their backs.

"How long is she planning to stay?" Ariel whispered to her father. "Look at all those suitcases!"

King Triton frowned. "I expect you to be polite, Ariel," he whispered back. "Remember, you are a princess—and my daughter!"

Pearl put her hands on her hips and looked around her. "Well, here I am," she

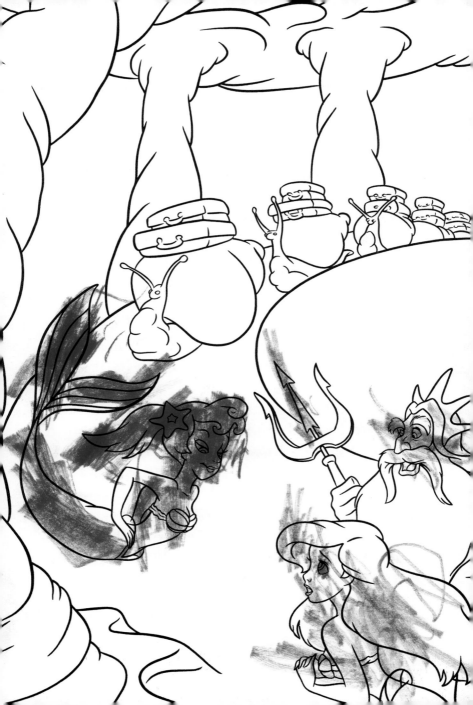

said. "Where should I put my things?"

King Triton came forward. "Welcome, Pearl," he said. "There's a spare bedroom next to Ariel's. She can show you where it is."

Ariel glared at her father.

"Thank you ever so much, King Triton," said Pearl. "I am just so looking forward to my stay here. I know that dear, dear Ariel and I will have a delightful time."

"I'm sure you will, too," Triton replied. He gave Ariel a meaningful glance that said *I expect you to be nice!*

Ariel turned to Pearl. "Come on," she said. "I'll show you to your room." Pearl snapped her fingers, and the parade of snails began to move again.

As Ariel and Pearl made their way toward the royal bedchambers, Pearl gazed around at the high ceilings and pink coral floors. "It's too bad you don't have a brother," she said. "Then I could marry him, become a princess, and live here forever!"

Ariel had often thought it would be fun to have a brother. Now she was glad she had no brother for Pearl to marry.

It took Pearl several hours to unpack all

her things. When she was done, she came into Ariel's room. "I'm ready," she said.

"Ready for what?" asked Ariel. She was lying on her bed, reading.

"For you to start showing me a good time, of course," replied Pearl.

"I'll be ready in a little while," Ariel said. "Right now, I want to finish this story."

Ariel went back to her book, but Pearl stayed in the doorway. She thumped her tail impatiently on the floor. Thump—thump—thump. "I'm waiting," she sang out.

Thump, thump, thump.

Ariel tried to read, but Pearl was being too annoying. Thump—thump—thump. Ariel couldn't pay attention to her reading with that constant thumping. "Oh, all right!" she said, slamming her book shut. "What do you want to do?"

"I want to meet your royal friends," said Pearl. She had drifted over to Ariel's mirror. She gazed at her face and smiled. Then she pinched her cheeks to make them rosier.

"My best friend is a fish, and he's not royal," Ariel told her.

"Yuck. I don't want to meet some finny

fish," Pearl said, sticking up her delicate nose.

"I have another friend named Gil. But he isn't royal, either."

Pearl's eyes brightened. "But he *is* a boy. That's a little more interesting."

"Come on," said Ariel.

With Ariel in the lead, the two girls swam out of the palace. After a few minutes, they reached a sea valley where triangular black rays swam in a group. Pearl shrank back from the odd creatures. "Is this your idea of a joke, Ariel?" she snapped. "Let's get away from these horrid creatures at once!"

Ariel swam among the rays, petting their velvety backs. "They won't hurt you," she told Pearl.

Just then a ray darted up from behind a coral reef. A young merman held on to its fins, letting the ray drag him through the water.

"Yahooo!" he cried. "Go, Sparky!" He let the ray pull him along until he spotted Ariel.

"Hi, Ariel!" he said, and let go of the ray.

"Hi, Gil," Ariel greeted her friend. "This is Pearl."

"Hello there, Gil," Pearl said, batting her

lashes. "It is such a total pleasure to meet you."

Gil looked at Ariel. His eyes asked a question: *Is she for real?* Ariel replied with a little shrug. Gil turned back to Pearl. "Nice to meet you, too," he said politely.

"It is so very brave of you to ride a ray," Pearl went on.

"Rays are friendly," said Gil. "They don't mind at all."

Just then a ray swam by. It brushed the side of Pearl's tail. "Eeeek!" she squealed, rolling her tail up. "Make it go away! Make it stop!"

"Venus was just saying hello," Gil explained.

"Oh, Gil, I do need you to protect me from these frightening things," said Pearl, floating very close to him. "I've never met anyone as brave as you."

Ariel covered her mouth, trying hard not to laugh. Gil looked at Pearl as if she were insane.

"Now, Gil, I want you to tell me all about yourself," Pearl flirted. "I'm sure you've had an amazing life."

"No, not really," Gil said.

"Nonsense! You must tell me all about it," Pearl insisted.

Ariel playfully crossed her eyes at Gil. With a sigh, Gil began to tell Pearl all about himself. Pearl floated close to him, resting her chin on her fingertips.

Suddenly Ariel heard a sound behind her. "Pssst! Pssst!"

Ariel turned and saw her best friend hiding behind a rock. "Flounder!" she said in a surprised whisper. "What are you doing here?"

"I came looking for you," the bright yellow-and-blue fish replied. "Come with me. I've found something you'll want to see."

Ariel glanced over at Pearl and Gil. Gil was busy talking, and Pearl was busy listening—or at least she was *pretending* to listen.

Quietly Ariel slipped off the rock and followed Flounder.

Flounder led Ariel over a coral ridge and down into another sea valley. "There it is," Flounder said, pointing with his fin.

A shiny brass chest lay at a slight tilt on the ocean floor. The ever-shifting sand had covered one side of it, and tiny barnacles had affixed themselves to the unburied side. "It looks like it's been here for a long time," Ariel noted as she swam down to it.

It took all of her strength, but Ariel finally pried the rusty lid open. The things inside sparkled up at her.

Reaching in gingerly, Ariel pulled out one of the sparkling things, then shut the chest. "What do you think it is?" she asked Flounder.

"I don't know," he replied, "but it's the strangest thing we've found yet! It looks like two small seashells framed and held together by a gold band. But these shells are so weird . . . you can see *through* them! I've never seen seashells you could see through before, have you?"

Ariel giggled with delight. "Maybe they're *see*shells. Get it?"

Flounder laughed at Ariel's joke. "Look at those thin bands sticking off the sides," he said. "What are they for?"

"I'm not sure," Ariel replied. "But they're curved at the tips. This *is* strange!"

The clear shells and their gold bands were so pretty that Ariel thought the treasure might be a human necklace. She tried to attach the two thin bands together behind her neck, but they wouldn't reach. "Perhaps humans have very thin necks," she considered.

Cracking the chest open again, Ariel took out a second treasure that looked very much like the first, only these clear shells were half circles and were connected by a thin blue band studded with small jewels. "Isn't this lovely," Ariel sighed.

"Maybe they're hats," Flounder suggested.

Ariel propped the gold-rimmed *see*shell treasure on top of Flounder's head. "It does look nice on you," she said. Just then it slipped forward, and the small band connecting the two shells settled on Flounder's nose. He was looking through the shells!

"Yoaw!" he cried, swimming in circles. "Everything looks gigantic. And blurry! Get these off me!" He shook his head until the *see*shells shook free and began floating away.

Ariel reached up and grabbed them back.

"One thing is for sure," said Flounder. "They *don't* go on your eyes. You can't see a thing with them over your eyes."

Ariel took the blue-rimmed shells and held them up to her eyes. She hooked the two curvy parts behind her ears. The middle rim rested on her nose. She looked through the clear shells. Everything seemed large and blurry.

"You're certainly right," Ariel agreed. "If you had to look through these," she said, "you'd

never know where you were going."

She put the treasures back into the chest and shut the lid tightly. "Maybe someday I'll find out what they are," she said with a sigh as she looked longingly up at the surface of the water. "But for now, these will be a *great* addition to my collection of human stuff! Let's take it to my secret treasure grotto right now."

Ariel pulled up on one handle. The chest was so deeply buried in the sand that it wouldn't budge.

"Now what?" asked Flounder.

Ariel thought. "I'll have to carry several armfuls at a time." She reopened the chest and scooped as many treasures as she could into her arms. Then she and Flounder swam toward the grotto.

Ariel had discovered the grotto a few years back, during one of her treasure hunts. With its high stone walls of shelves that the strong sea currents had carved through the years, Ariel decided the artificial cave was the perfect place to hide her collection of land treasures. Because the entrance was hidden by an enormous boulder, no one but Ariel and Flounder knew of its existence.

When they reached the grotto, Ariel went inside to get a large fishing net that she'd found on a wrecked boat. "We can put the human shell things in here," she said.

"But then it will be too heavy to carry," Flounder noted.

Ariel thought for a moment. "We'll just have to carry over a little bit at a time," she said. "Then we can store them in the net."

Ariel and Flounder made several trips carting the treasures to the grotto. As they worked, Ariel told Flounder about Pearl. "She sounds terrible," said Flounder.

"She is," Ariel agreed.

"I wish I could tell Father about this wonderful treasure," Ariel said as they headed back to the chest. "But he just wouldn't understand."

"He thinks he's protecting you by forbidding you to collect land treasures," Flounder reminded her. "He's afraid you'll go to the surface and be captured by humans."

"But I don't think the humans would capture me," Ariel said. "I'm sure they're really good at heart. Creatures who make such beautiful things *must* be good.

"I wish Father would change his rule about collecting land treasures," Ariel continued. "I love land things so much, I can't stop myself from collecting them. These human thingamabobs you found today are so great!"

Suddenly Ariel gasped.

There was Pearl, sitting beside their netful of treasures!

"I heard that remark," Pearl said, swooshing her tail from side to side. "Human thingamabobs, eh? So that's what these are. I was wondering."

Ariel's eyes darted to the entryway to her grotto. It looked like just a crack in the boulder. Had Pearl discovered it? How much had she seen?

"Everyone knows King Triton's rule about collecting land objects," Pearl went on. "How shocking that the king's very own daughter is breaking the rule."

"Pearl, I . . . um . . . uh," Ariel stammered. "Where is Gil?"

Pearl's eyes narrowed meanly. "He left. And so did you! I don't like being ditched, Ariel. Do you think that just because you're a princess you can swim away from me?"

She did not wait for Ariel to answer. "You

don't even care about being a princess," Pearl continued. "You have no respect for the title. *I* should have been the princess. At least I know how to act like royalty."

"Pearl . . ." Ariel said nervously, "I . . . I thought you were busy with Gil. I didn't think you'd mind."

"Well, I did mind."

"How much have you seen?" Flounder blurted out.

"Everything. I've seen every bit of it," Pearl replied, glaring at Ariel.

"Everything?" gasped Ariel. Then Pearl *had* seen the grotto!

"I saw you bring that last bunch of these things here, so I waited for you to come back. Now I've caught you red-handed! Wait until I tell King Triton what you've been up to!"

"You wouldn't!" Ariel gasped. "Oh, please, Pearl. I'll do anything you say. Anything! Just please don't tell my father."

Pearl looked sharply at Ariel. "*Anything* I say?" she asked.

"Yes," Ariel repeated wearily. "Anything."

Aquata stuck her head out of her bedroom doorway. It was early the next morning. "Ariel!" she demanded. "Whatever are you doing?"

Ariel stopped and balanced the tray of covered dishes she was carrying. "I'm bringing Pearl breakfast," she said.

"Why?" Aquata asked.

"Uh, I want Pearl to feel welcome," Ariel replied.

Aquata regarded her sister suspiciously. "Is

that why you were polishing her nails and picking her things up off the floor last night?" she asked.

"Sure," said Ariel.

Aquata put her hands on her hips. "I don't believe you."

"Believe what you like," said Ariel, trying to sound unconcerned. "But Father asked me to make sure Pearl was having a pleasurable stay. I'm only trying to follow his wishes!"

Ariel continued down the hall. She could feel Aquata staring after her. She knew her sisters thought she was acting strange. And they were right—she was. Since the moment she and Pearl had returned to the palace the day before, Ariel had been swimming around serving Pearl's every wish. She'd lent Pearl her favorite coral necklace and cleaned Pearl's clothes. She'd fetched a cool drink for Pearl when she complained of being thirsty and got her a blanket when she grumbled about being cold. Pearl had no trouble thinking of an endless stream of things for Ariel to do.

"Fluff up my pillow after you set down the

tray," ordered Pearl when Ariel came into her room. Ariel sighed and fluffed up the pillow.

"And while I'm eating, you may brush my hair."

Brush her hair? This is too much, Ariel thought. Do this, do that, bring me this, bring me that. Ariel couldn't take it anymore. "Listen here, Pearl," she said. "You'd just better cut it out. I'm not going to—"

"I know a little secret . . . I know a little secret," Pearl sang.

Ariel bit her lip to keep from saying something nasty. Without a word, she spun around, grabbed a brush from the dressing table, and ran it roughly through Pearl's hair. "Ouch!" Pearl cried. "Gently, please!"

"So sorry, Pearl," Ariel grumbled.

"Oh, and Ariel, after breakfast, I wish to ride the royal sea horses," Pearl stated.

"Do you know how to ride?" Ariel asked.

"No, but you'll teach me," answered Pearl.

Ariel swam out into the hallway. She tightened her fingers into fists. "Oooh! I'd like to . . . to . . ."

"What's the matter, Ariel?" asked Adella as she glided past. "You look angry about something."

"Nothing, nothing at all," Ariel answered with a forced smile. When Adella was gone, Ariel swam down to the dining room. If only she could tell her sisters the truth! Maybe they would know how to deal with Pearl.

After breakfast, Ariel took Pearl to the royal stables. "Good morning, Princess Ariel," said Mackey, the merman in charge of the stables.

"My . . . uh . . . friend Pearl wants to learn how to ride," Ariel told him. "Do you have a nice, tame sea horse for her?"

Mackey swam to a stall and returned with a gentle white sea horse. "Foamy is a sweet one," he said.

But Pearl pointed to a golden sea horse nearby. "I want him," she demanded.

"That's Wildride," said Mackey. "And his name says it all."

"Why don't you try Foamy," Ariel said.

"I don't want that old sea hag," Pearl frowned. "I *want* Wildride. Do you understand, Ariel?"

Ariel clenched her teeth. "Certainly, Pearl *dear,* whatever you say."

Ariel led Crystal, her favorite sea horse, out into the corral. A fence made from sand logs and covered with netting surrounded the area where Ariel and her sisters usually rode their sea horses. A net attached to four posts floated above them to keep the sea horses from swimming out of the area.

Ariel left Crystal and went back into the stable for Wildride. The beautiful sea horse backed up when she got near. "Easy, boy," Ariel said, petting his head. "You ready to go for a ride today?"

Wildride seemed to understand her. He settled down and let Ariel lead him out. Pearl swam after them. "You be careful on that horse, miss," Mackey said to Pearl.

"Oh, I will," Pearl replied sweetly in the voice she always used with grown-ups.

A few minutes later Mackey led the other sea horses into the corral. "I guess she'll be all right as long as *you* stay inside the fence," Mackey said to Ariel. "I'll keep an eye on her while I let these other sea horses get some exercise."

"Thanks," said Ariel.

To Ariel's surprise, Pearl did pretty well with Wildride. As they rode slowly around the corral, Ariel called out to Pearl. "Sit forward a little more," she suggested.

Pearl scooted forward. "This is so easy," she said, her nose in the air.

"I'm going to collect some seaweed to feed the critters," said Mackey. "You girls just take it slow till I come back."

Mackey went out the corral gate, locking it behind him. The herd of sea horses floated peacefully. "Thank goodness he's gone," said Pearl. "Now we can have some *fun!*" She reached behind her and slapped Wildride's side. "Come on, Wildride. Let's see what you can do!"

"Pearl, be careful!" Ariel shouted.

With an angry whinny, Wildride began swimming backward, trying to shake Pearl off. His curled tail shot out behind him as he backed up into the fence. Crash! A top rung of the fence came falling down.

"Don't pull back on his reins!" Ariel yelled.

But Pearl wasn't listening. She was so

scared that she pulled back on the reins even tighter. Wildride whinnied and backed into the fence again. This time he knocked two rungs from the fence.

"Help!" screamed Pearl. She'd lost hold of the reins. She clung to Wildride's neck, terrified.

"Just let go!" cried Ariel. "You'll float right up."

But Pearl was frozen with fear. "I can't let go," she whimpered. "I'm scared."

Just then Wildride saw that there was an opening in the fence. He bolted through it at top speed. "Stop him!" Pearl screeched.

"Come on, Crystal!" said Ariel. She rode through the break in the fence. Wildride and Pearl were just ahead of them.

"Let go!" Ariel yelled again. She leaned forward and loosened Crystal's reins, a signal for her sea horse to go faster. Suddenly the sound of wild whinnying made Ariel check over her shoulder.

All the sea horses were swimming through the break in the fence!

"Oh, no!" she cried.

"Help!" shrieked Pearl.

"Faster, Crystal! Faster!" Ariel urged her sea horse on until she was side by side with Wildride and Pearl.

"Make him stop!" Pearl yelped.

"Just let go!" Ariel told her one more time.

"I can't! I'm too scared!"

Reaching across, Ariel grabbed Pearl's arm. She pried it loose. Then she yanked at Pearl's other arm.

When Pearl's arms were loosened from

Wildride's neck, she floated up and away from the sea horse. Free, Wildride swam away over a coral ridge.

Working the reins, Ariel turned Crystal around. The herd of sea horses was charging straight at them! She yelled to Pearl, "Hop on!"

"Up, Crystal! Swim up!" she commanded the sea horse, pulling the reins back gently. Just in time, Crystal floated up over the charging herd. In an instant, the herd followed Wildride over the ridge.

"What took you so long to save me?" Pearl demanded.

"Took me so long!" Ariel gasped. "Why didn't you just let go when I told you to?"

Pearl folded her arms and looked away. "Because I might have been thrown! I could have crashed into something," she huffed.

"No, you would have just floated up," Ariel told her.

"Well, that's not the point. You were supposed to be looking out for me," Pearl insisted.

"Pearl!" Ariel cried. "Do you realize what just happened?"

"I was almost killed!" Pearl snapped back.

"No you weren't! We just let loose the entire herd of royal sea horses! Do you know what my father will—"

At that moment Mackey rode up to them. "Are you girls all right?" he asked.

"We're fine," said Ariel.

"Speak for yourself," said Pearl, rubbing her wrist. "I was nearly—"

"We're fine," Ariel repeated. "But the sea horses all swam over that ridge."

"Oh my gosh!" Mackey cried. "How did this happen?"

"Well . . . um . . . it was," Ariel stammered. She didn't like telling on anyone, not even Pearl. She looked at Pearl, hoping the guilty mermaid might confess on her own. But Pearl floated silently by and didn't say a word.

"Never mind," Mackey said impatiently. "I've got to get them back. The king will be furious! I'd better get some help." He turned his sea horse around and rode back toward the stable.

"I *told* you to take Foamy," Ariel said to Pearl.

"Hmmph," Pearl replied, then swam off without waiting for Ariel.

With a sigh, Ariel swam back toward the stables, but suddenly she stopped short. Ahead of her, Pearl was talking to King Triton. Triton's arms were folded, and his face was red with anger.

Maybe *now* he would begin to understand what a troublemaker Pearl really was, Ariel thought.

She hurried over to them. "I guess Pearl told you what happened," she said to her father.

"She certainly did!" Triton boomed. "Ariel, how could you be so irresponsible?"

"Me?" cried Ariel.

"Don't deny it," said Triton. "Pearl told me how you were showing off, trying to get Crystal to swim faster."

"It was awful," Pearl piped in, feigning a look of horror. "Crystal went so fast he crashed right through the fence!"

"Didn't you notice the other sea horses escaping, Ariel?" Triton asked. "Or did you just not care?"

"I *did* care, Father," Ariel tried to explain.

"It was just that I had to go get Pearl because—" Ariel stopped short.

Pearl had drifted behind Triton and was smiling an evil little smile. She folded her arms across her chest and stared at Ariel with narrowed eyes.

"Because why?" asked King Triton.

"Because . . . because . . . because no reason." Ariel hung her head. "I'm sorry, Father."

"I'm very disappointed in you, Ariel. I don't like this kind of recklessness. I want you to spend the next few hours in your room thinking about what you've done."

For the rest of the day Ariel sat at her bedroom window and watched as Mackey rounded up the sea horses. One by one, the stable hands rode them in. It was a long time before Mackey returned with the last one.

Ariel turned away from her window. Someone was tapping at her bedroom door. "Come in," she called.

"All right, Ariel," Sebastian said as he came into the room. "What *really* happened?"

Ariel's heart ached. She longed to tell Sebastian the truth. She didn't want everyone thinking she had done such a thoughtless thing. But Sebastian would never understand about her treasures. He had no patience for anything to do with humans.

"It was just like Pearl said," Ariel lied. "I crashed through the fence. Then I just kept riding."

"I don't believe you!" Sebastian scoffed. "You are forgetful, yes. Headstrong, yes. Stubborn as a barnacle, yes. . . ."

"What's your point?" Ariel asked.

"That you would not do something mean and careless like this."

"Thanks, Sebastian," said Ariel.

"What really happened?" Sebastian asked again.

"That's what really happened," Ariel said. "It was all my fault."

"Ariel," Sebastian said. "Don't clam up on me. Is that Pearl really as sweet as she seems? Or is there a merdevil hiding behind that smiling face?"

"She's really very sweet." Ariel had to force out the words.

Sebastian shook his head sadly. "If you say

so," he said. Still shaking his head, Sebastian left the room.

That night Ariel didn't go to dinner. She did not want to see anyone—especially Pearl. She read for a while and then went to bed. The only good thing about this day had been that she'd gotten away from Pearl for several hours.

Ariel was in a deep sleep when something woke her up. It was a finger poking into her shoulder. She opened her eyes and saw Pearl standing beside her bed.

Ariel sat up. "It's the middle of the night, Pearl. What do you want?"

"Shhhh!" Pearl hissed. "We're sneaking out of here. I want to see Eel-Ectric City."

"Eel-Ectric City!" Ariel cried.

"Shhhh," said Pearl. "Do you know how to get there?"

"Yes, but I don't want to go there at night. It's too dangerous."

"Don't be a baby!" said Pearl. "I've heard it's very exciting there. And you're going to take me."

"I am not," said Ariel.

"I guess I'll just have to go down the hall

and wake up King Triton, then," said Pearl as she turned toward the door. "I have something very interesting to tell him. It's all about a bunch of human things his very own daughter has found."

Pearl turned to leave.

"Wait!" Ariel stopped her. "Okay, okay, I'll go with you. It seems I have no choice."

"We're lost! I know we're lost!" Pearl cried. She pointed a finger in Ariel's face. "And it's all *your* fault!"

Ariel had never been to this dark, cold part of the ocean before. She cocked her head and listened, trying to make out a faint sound in the distance.

"What? What is it?" Pearl asked. "What do you hear? Is something coming?"

"It's music," Ariel said. She followed the sound until she came to the end of a black cliff. Looking down, she saw a city ablaze with lights. The music was drifting up from the city.

Eel-Ectric City.

Pearl swam up beside her. "Wow!" she gasped. "It's just like I pictured!"

Pearl swam down to the city as fast as she could. Ariel followed, wishing she were home in bed—anyplace but *here*. If her father discovered they'd gone to Eel-Ectric City in the middle of the night, he'd be furious.

Still . . . it *was* a tiny bit exciting, Ariel thought as they entered the city. She had never seen so many lights before. There were signs lit up everywhere. Some signs had glowing eels forming the letters of words. Other signs had multicolored eels slithering up and down poles so that the words seemed to wiggle colorfully.

Down in the shell-lined streets, merpeople swam about as if it were day. The music was loud now, blaring from the different doorways the mermaids passed.

Ariel and Pearl stopped in the middle of one street. "What should we do now?" Ariel asked. Before Pearl could answer, Ariel felt a tap on her shoulder. The long tentacle of an octopus was reaching out from a slightly open door. The tentacle was covered with bangle bracelets. The bangles jingled as the tentacle did a twisting, curvy dance around them. Then, with its tip, it beckoned the girls to follow it inside.

"Let's go in," Pearl said eagerly.

Ariel grabbed her shoulder. "Stop, Pearl! I don't like the look of this place."

At that moment a loud siren filled the air. A sea-horse-drawn wagon zoomed up to the building, its blowfish wailing out the shrill siren sound. Merpolice in tall blue caps swam alongside the wagon.

"I think we should be going," said Ariel. She pulled Pearl down the road. Over her shoulder Ariel saw the merpolice pulling merpeople from the building and putting them in the police wagon. Ariel was glad they hadn't gone inside.

"Let's go in here," said Pearl, pointing to a doorway in front of them. Ariel looked at the sign in the curtained window. Small purple eels formed the words: Tina's Teahouse. Tea Sold. Fortunes Told.

Pearl rushed into the building before Ariel could protest. Not wanting to be left alone, Ariel had no choice but to follow.

Inside, the lights were dim. Purple eels glided along the ceiling, casting a lavender glow over everything. Merfolk sat at tables, sipping cups of spicy urchin tea from clamshell cups.

On a small stage, a band of sole fish played soft, dreamy music. One blew through a conch shell. Another used the back of a sea tortoise as a drum. The third shook two closed oystershells. Their pearls rattled inside.

A fat, heavily made-up merwoman with purple hair moved from table to table, her long robe flowing behind her. Her many bracelets and rings jingled as she walked.

The woman made her way over to Ariel and Pearl. "I am Miss Rosa," she said. Her voice was low and smooth. "Care to have your fortunes told, ladies?"

"No thank you," said Ariel at the same time that Pearl said, "Sure."

Miss Rosa took Pearl's hand. "Very soft," she noted. She closed her eyes. "I'm sensing something," she said. "Yes!" Her eyes snapped open. "The sea spirits have told me that you do not like to work."

"That's right!" Pearl squealed with delight. "You *are* good at this."

Miss Rosa drew Pearl along. "Come with me to my private table. I will tell you more—all that the future has in store. Only three sand dollars for the first four minutes."

Ariel watched Pearl disappear behind a curtain with Miss Rosa. She sat down to wait. A barracuda in a black beret swam over and asked if she wanted to order tea. "No thanks," she said.

With her chin propped in her hands, Ariel waited. She hoped Pearl wouldn't be long.

Two mermen sat at the next table. One was young with a short beard; the other was much older. The older one's flowing gray hair was pulled back in a braid. Ariel's table was so close to the mermen's that she could hear everything they were saying.

"My grandfather told me this story, so I know it's true," said the older merman. "The golden ship will arrive in three days. It sails to the underwater tip of an island in the middle of the Anemone Valley once every hundred years. They drop anchor and throw things into the sea."

"What kinds of things?" asked the younger merman.

"Human things—small, round, flat things made of gold and silver. My grandfather said the things have pictures of human kings and queens on them. The humans sacrifice their treasures as an offering to the sea so that it will stay calm and not rise up and flood their land."

"Will you be there?" asked the younger merman.

"No," the older merman replied. "Their things aren't worth anything to us."

The mermen paid for their tea and left. Ariel couldn't believe what she had heard. She hadn't known about these things that had pictures of human kings and queens on them! How wonderful!

Ariel didn't care that the things had no value under the sea. She just *had* to see them. What did human kings and queens look like? Ariel made up her mind: She was going to see those pictures no matter what!

Anemone Valley had the largest field of anemones in the entire ocean. It was far away, but Ariel could make it if she left the palace early in the morning.

Suddenly she heard shouting from behind the curtain. Pearl stormed out, and Miss Rosa raced after her.

"What happened?" asked Ariel, jumping up.

"That fat sea cow can't read fortunes," Pearl cried. "She said I would marry a giant squid and spend the rest of my life cleaning his house."

"I don't make these things up," said Miss Rosa. "I just say what I see." She pointed to the small purse Pearl wore around her wrist. "And I expect three sand dollars!"

"Forget it," said Pearl. "I'd pay you for a real fortune! But not for that fortune. You just made it up."

Ariel glanced up. She noticed that the eels along the wall had stopped moving. They had picked up their skinny heads and were staring down at the girls. "Pay her, Pearl," Ariel whispered.

"No way. I expect value for my money," Pearl insisted.

"Get them!" screeched Miss Rosa. At that moment the eels swam down the wall. They were headed right for Ariel and Pearl!

Ariel grabbed Pearl's arm. "Let's go!" As they swam out the front door, Ariel felt something brush against her tail. The eels were right behind them!

Ariel and Pearl darted around a corner, the eels right on their tails. In a matter of seconds, the slimy creatures would be upon them.

Two barrels stood against the wall of a nearby building. "Quick! Climb in," Ariel told Pearl. In a flash, both mermaids were crouched down inside a barrel. Ariel looked up and saw a flurry of bubbles above her head as the eels zoomed past. She waited for the bubbles to stop.

Slowly Ariel lifted her head up. "The coast is clear," she said.

Pearl peered fearfully around in all directions. "Are you sure?" she asked.

"I don't see anyone," Ariel said, and floated up out of the barrel. Bits of green seaweed clung to her skin and hair. She sniffed its sour scent. "Oh, yuck, pickled seaweed," she said, picking pieces from her hair.

"Only *you* would pick pickled seaweed barrels to hide in," said Pearl, plucking seaweed off her arms.

Ariel put her hands on her hips. "I didn't know there was anything in the barrels! Besides, we got away from the eels. That's the important thing."

"I don't like this place," said Pearl. "I want to go back to the palace."

"Thank goodness," Ariel sighed.

Keeping a sharp lookout for the eels, the girls swam through Eel-Ectric City back toward the black and silent part of the ocean. Ariel did her best to remember the way back, but it wasn't long before they were lost.

"I thought you knew the way," Pearl

whined after they had been swimming for a long time.

"Listen, Pearl!" Ariel shouted. "I'm tired! My hair stinks of pickled seaweed! And now I'm completely lost! And it's all because of you."

"It wasn't my fault that woman couldn't tell fortunes. I was not about to pay her," Pearl replied.

Ariel stared at Pearl for a moment.

"Why are you doing this to me, Pearl?" she finally asked.

"Because I want to see what it feels like to be you," said Pearl. "You're a princess. You get to do whatever you like."

"What?" Ariel cried. "No I don't. Why would you even think such a thing?"

"Of course you do. Everyone talks about it. Princess Ariel just goes off and does as she pleases. That's what they all say. *I* can't do that. I have to stay at home and listen to my mother all day. She tells me what to say, what to do, how to dress. This is my chance to have wild adventures like you do. It's my chance to *be* you."

"But I don't do wild things," said Ariel.

"Then tell me exactly how you spend your days," Pearl insisted.

Ariel didn't want to tell Pearl any more than she already knew. "I just swim around," she said.

Pearl snorted with laughter. "Oh, sure. Tell me another. You have a great life. You have adventures and servants waiting on you hand and foot. It's not fair that you have those things and I don't. I'm much more princesslike than you are. My hair is nicer, I'm more delicate, I don't hang around with fish." Pearl's eyes narrowed. "And I don't collect human treasures."

"All right, Pearl," Ariel gave in wearily. "What if you *are* more princesslike than I am? That's not my fault."

"Perhaps not, but it's still unfair. I'm just evening things up a bit. Now *I* have a servant—you! And we'll have all the adventures I say we're going to have."

As she spoke, Ariel saw the top of the palace looming above a hill. They were much closer to home than she'd thought. She was glad, because it was nearly morning.

Suddenly Ariel saw a figure coming over

the hill. Who would be up so early? she wondered. Then her heart began to pound. Even at a distance, she knew those broad shoulders and that regal bearing.

"It's my father!" she gasped.

Pearl whirled around. "Uh-oh."

At that moment Triton spotted the girls. He rushed to them joyfully. "Ariel!" he cried. "I was so worried. I didn't know what happened. Are you all right?"

Pearl spoke up before Ariel could answer. "I saw that Ariel wasn't in her bed, so I came out to find her," she said. "She was in Eel-Ectric City, and I made her come back."

"Eel-Ectric City!" Triton shouted. "In the middle of the night!"

"No, Father. That's not true," Ariel replied.

"No? Then what is *that*?" Triton demanded, pointing to Ariel's tail. It shimmered with an eerie purple light. Ariel hadn't noticed that when her tail fin had touched the purple eel, some eel scales had brushed off onto her.

"The Eel-Ectric City part is true, but . . ." Ariel stopped in midsentence. Triton was lobster red with anger. To Ariel, he looked twice his normal size. When he spoke, it was in a low, calm voice. Too calm.

"Ariel, this time you have indeed gone too far. You swim straight to your room, young lady. As of now, you are grounded for two weeks!"

Ariel almost burst into tears. Two weeks! That meant she would miss the golden ship! She hung her head and started to make her way back to the palace. "Yes, Father," she said sadly.

But before she swam away, Ariel sneaked a look at Pearl, who was standing close behind the King. Ariel had the sudden urge to slap that smug smile right off Pearl's obnoxious face!

Two days later, Ariel was slowly swimming past the music room on her way upstairs. Sebastian noticed her and came scurrying after her. "All right, Ariel, *what is going on?*" he asked.

"Nothing is going on, Sebastian," she replied.

"I know better than that," Sebastian insisted. "You've never left the palace in the middle of the night before. It's that Pearl, isn't it? Just give me the word, Ariel. Tell me that it's Pearl causing all this trouble and I'll go right to your father and talk to him!"

"Please don't say anything to him," said Ariel.

"Then *you* talk to him," Sebastian urged her. "Tell him right now what is going on. Your father is leaving on a business trip this afternoon. If you don't talk to him now, you won't get the chance till tomorrow evening."

"There's nothing to tell," insisted Ariel, covering her mouth as she yawned. "I'm so tired," she said. "Excuse me, but I need to sleep."

Ariel left Sebastian gazing after her as she went up to her bedroom and shut the door.

Ariel flopped down on her bed and tried to think things through. She had only two choices. One was to tell her father the truth and risk losing her treasure grotto. The other was to be at Pearl's mercy forever. Either way, her life would be unbearable!

And now it looked as if she would miss the golden ship. There was no way to get there if she was grounded. Suddenly Ariel remembered what Sebastian had said: *Your father is leaving on a business trip this afternoon.*

"I'll sneak out early tomorrow morning," Ariel said out loud. "No one will know. And I'll be back before he returns."

The next morning, Ariel awoke with a start. She got out of bed and looked out her window. The sea was calm and still. I must be the only mermaid awake at this hour, she thought. Quietly she left her room and went into the hall. It was nearly silent in the royal bedchambers. The only sounds were the little snores coming from Adella's room. As she passed Pearl's room, Ariel peeked in. She wanted to make sure Pearl was asleep. She didn't need that nasty mermaid spoiling things for her yet again.

Pearl had the covers pulled up over her head. Good, thought Ariel. She's sound asleep.

Ariel left the palace and began to swim quickly. She had never been to Anemone Valley, but she had an idea where it was.

After Ariel had been swimming for hours, she noticed that the water had grown warmer. This told her she was heading south, in the right direction.

Suddenly Ariel stopped short. She saw

purple, red, and green tentacles hanging down in front of her. She knew right away that it was a Portuguese man-of-war! Sebastian had told her many times about the man-of-war and how its tentacles were poisonous.

Ariel tried to swim past it as quietly as she could, taking quick glances at the waving tentacles above her. Just when she was almost out of its reach, she heard a deep, full voice call to her.

"Halt!"

Ariel looked up sharply.

"You! Mermaid! What is your business in my waters? I have never seen you before."

"I am Princess Ariel," she said, trying to sound unafraid.

"Hah!" he scoffed. "I don't believe you. Come closer."

Ariel moved toward him, trying to stay clear of his floating tentacles. "Am I near Anemone Valley?" she asked bravely.

"Why would a princess be going there?" the man-of-war questioned suspiciously.

"I'm on a royal mission for my father, King Triton," Ariel fibbed, hoping he'd stop asking her questions. "It's most important that I get there."

The man-of-war regarded her carefully. "You are quite near," he said, his voice less harsh. "Continue swimming south until you come to a large pink rock. The rock is the tip of an island. Next to it is Anemone Valley."

"The tip of an island! That's exactly the part of the valley I'm looking for," said Ariel. "Thank you very much."

Ariel continued swimming south until she came to the rocky pink tip of the island. Sloping down beside it was a huge group of tiny green-and-orange-striped anemones. The strange sea creatures drew in their flowerlike tentacles as Ariel arrived. Ariel looked at them and smiled. "Don't worry. I won't hurt you."

Ariel looked up. She'd made it! The golden ship would be along any moment. All she had to do now was wait.

She settled in on the pink rock. At that moment a pod of dolphins swam into sight. They jumped to the surface, then plunged down again into the water.

As the dolphins came closer, Ariel saw that

someone was hanging on to the tail fin of the last one.

It was Pearl!

Ariel was stunned. She watched open-mouthed as Pearl let go of the dolphin's fin and swam toward her. "If that darn dolphin leapt up one more time, I think I would have lost my mind," Pearl griped, settling in on the rock beside Ariel.

"How did you get here?" Ariel asked in disbelief. "Why are you here?"

Pearl smiled smugly. "You are not getting rid of me that easily. You woke me when you came into my room. I'm really a very light sleeper, you know. I've been following you since you left the palace. I don't believe you actually talked to that man-of-war. What a disgusting creature. I heard you tell it you were going to Anemone Valley. I was here last year during one of Mother and Father's dreadful vacations."

Ariel put her hands over her face and sighed. Would she ever be free of Pearl?

"If you think you could go off on an adventure and leave me out, you are dead wrong," Pearl continued. "I told you, Ariel, I don't like to be ditched." She smoothed down her scales and primped her hair. "So, why are we here?'

Ariel's mind was working hard. She could still race away and try to give Pearl the slip. But then she would miss the ship.

Just then a shadow fell over them. "A ship!" Pearl cried, looking up. "You knew this was coming, didn't you?"

Ariel threw up her arms. What was the use of lying? Pearl would find out what was going on soon, anyway. "Yes, it's a ship. The humans are going to throw some things overboard. It's a ceremony of some sort."

Pearl's eyes sparkled with greed. She looked sharply at Ariel. "If there's anything good, it's mine!"

Pearl couldn't even wait for the humans to throw their objects overboard. She began to swim toward the surface. Her greedy little hands were all ready to snatch up the treasures as soon as she saw them.

Disgusted, Ariel flicked a shell off the rock. She glanced up at Pearl.

"You really think I'm stupid, don't you, Ariel," Pearl called down, swimming upward as she spoke. "You're always trying to trick me. Well, we'll just see who has the last laugh."

Suddenly Ariel sat up straight. Something had fallen into the water. Only it wasn't a treasure.

"Pearl, look out!" Ariel screamed. "It's a *net!*"

"Yeah, sure. You can't scare me," Pearl laughed scornfully, still looking down at Ariel.

With a haughty swoosh of her tail fin Pearl turned around. But it was too late.

Pearl let out a terrified cry as she became entangled in the thick web of a fisherman's net!

Ariel froze in horror as she watched Pearl struggle. "Help!" Pearl screamed. "Ariel! Help me!"

For just a tiny split second, a nasty thought crossed Ariel's mind. If Pearl were gone, Ariel's troubles would be over.

But, of course, Ariel couldn't let that happen. She swam as hard and as fast as she could toward Pearl. "Get me out of here!" Pearl screeched. Ariel pulled on the net, trying to tear it, but the rope was too thick.

Just then she realized they were going up. The net was being pulled in!

With all her strength, Ariel pulled again on the net, but it was no use. With a quick, strong tug, the net was yanked from her hand.

"Ariel!" Pearl cried.

"Oh my gosh!" Ariel gasped. What could she do now?

At that moment a familiar voice called to her. "Ariel! Now what in the world are you up to?"

"Sebastian!" Ariel turned toward the crab. What is he doing here? she thought. But there was no time to ask. "Pearl is trapped in a fisherman's net!" she called, and pointed up. Pearl was being lifted completely out of the water.

"Grab a razor clamshell from the sea-floor," Sebastian shouted. Ariel swooped down and grabbed one of the long, sharp shells. Then she swam back to Sebastian, and they paddled to the surface.

With a gulp, Ariel broke through the water. Above her, Pearl hung in the net, dangling from the side of a large ship. Ariel reached up, but the net was too high.

"It's no use," moaned Sebastian. Just then Ariel remembered the dolphins—the way they leapt high out of the water. Ariel had always wanted to try leaping the way the dolphins did. Now was the time.

She tucked the razor shell into her belt purse and began to swim. It was important that she get up enough speed to make the leap. When she was moving as fast as she could, she lifted her head and slapped the water with her tail fin.

The next thing Ariel knew, she was sailing through the air! She reached out for the net, but her hand just brushed by it.

Whoosh! Ariel was back in the water. She flipped in a circle and began swimming back to leap again. This time she managed to grab hold of the netting with her fingers.

"Get me out, Ariel!" Pearl screamed frantically.

"Hold still," Ariel said. With her free hand, she fumbled for the razor shell. "I'll cut you loose."

It was hard working with one hand. Ariel had to curl her tail up and hook her tail fin

into a section of net. That helped her hang on.

"Faster! Faster!" Pearl yelled.

"You can do it, Ariel!" Sebastian called from below.

Ariel worked as quickly as she could. The strands of net thinned, then popped apart. "It's coming, Pearl," she said. "I'll have you out of here in no time."

Ariel wrapped both hands around either side of the opening she'd cut in the net. "Jump up and down!" she told Pearl.

Pearl began bouncing in the net. Ariel tugged and tugged.

Riiip! Finally, the net gave way, and Pearl tumbled out. For a second, Ariel dangled. Then she let herself drop.

Splash! Ariel and Pearl plunged back into the water. "Come on, girls!" Sebastian yelled to them as he paddled back down underwater. "Let's get out of here before the humans spot us."

As Sebastian spoke, another net was thrown into the water. It just missed him. The three of them kept low to the ocean floor and swam away as fast as they could.

When they could no longer see the shadow of the boat, they stopped on a rock to rest.

"How did you find me, Sebastian?" Ariel asked when she'd caught her breath.

"I was up all night worrying about you," he explained. "Then, early this morning I looked out my window and saw you sneaking out. I came running out after you, but you were too far ahead. I paddled as hard as I could, but I lost sight of you after a while. If I hadn't paid a stingray five sand dollars to carry me, I never would have made it!"

"But how did you know where I was going?" Ariel asked.

"I ran into an old friend of mine, Mano the man-of-war. He told me you were heading for Anemone Valley. Now *I* have a question. What are *you* doing here, Ariel?"

"I wanted to see the golden ship," Ariel said. But she told Sebastian only half the story. She left out the part about the treasures with the pictures of the kings and queens on them. "I heard it was supposed to be a great golden ship that comes once every hundred years. But it wasn't. It was just a fishing boat."

"No kidding," Pearl grumbled.

Sebastian shook his head wearily. "How many times do we have to go through this, Ariel? *Stay away from humans!* For a minute there, I thought you were going to *let* yourself be captured just to see them up close!"

"It didn't seem like the best way to meet them," Ariel admitted.

"There is no best way, child! Get that through your head!"

"That's what I've been trying to tell her," said Pearl.

Sebastian floated up and looked Pearl straight in the eye. "As for you, missy," he said, "I don't know what you are doing here. And you are not my business. But I do know that Ariel saved your life. Even after you've been making her miserable. I think it's time for you to say thanks!"

Pearl folded her arms and pouted. "Thank you," she mumbled.

"A little better than that!" Sebastian insisted.

"It's okay, Sebastian," Ariel said. "I think

that is the best Pearl can do."

Sebastian glared at Pearl. "Come on," he said.

"Maybe we can get home before the King returns. Then he need never know of this."

The three swam silently for a while, but Sebastian soon fell behind the girls. He couldn't keep up with their quick pace. When he was out of earshot, Pearl spoke. "So much for your wonderful humans!"

"Those were mean ones," Ariel said. "But they're not all mean. I'm sure of that."

"How can you be sure?" Pearl scoffed. "A bunch of weird human thingamabobs that you can see through doesn't tell you anything about humans."

"But what about all the other things?" Ariel asked.

"What other things?"

Ariel looked at Pearl. All at once she realized that Pearl knew only about the clear pairs of shells. Pearl couldn't tell King Triton about the grotto because she didn't know about it. She had never even seen it!

Ariel spun happily in the water.

"What's gotten into you?" Pearl muttered.

"Oh, nothing!" Ariel said, smiling. "Nothing at all!"

Not wanting to leave Sebastian too far behind, Ariel forced herself not to race ahead. But it was hard. There was something she wanted to do, and she couldn't wait to get to it.

By the time they returned to the palace, it was late afternoon. "The royal chariot is still gone," Sebastian noted, panting with exhaustion. "Your father is still out. Now, Ariel, be a good girl and—"

"I'll be home in a moment, Sebastian," Ariel said.

"Ariel! *Now* what—"

"Be right back!" Ariel called over her shoulder.

Just as Ariel had hoped, Pearl trailed after her. Ariel swam to the front of her treasure grotto. The clear shells were right there in the net, where she'd left them.

In a minute, Pearl caught up to her. "What are you doing?" she demanded. Ariel grabbed the net with a sudden burst of strength she didn't know she had and began swimming toward the surface.

"You'll see!" Ariel called back happily. She swam up until she was nearly to the top. "Watch this, Pearl!"

Ariel yanked open the net and let her prized treasures float to the top. In minutes, they were bobbing along the surface.

"What are you doing?" Pearl gasped.

"I'm not supposed to have these, so I'm sending them back to the surface," said Ariel. She watched the clear shells float. From below they looked like small jellyfish rimmed with shining gold and colored bands. A pang of sadness hit her. They were so lovely, she hated to give them up.

But it was a small price to pay for her freedom. "They're gone, Pearl," she said. "You can't threaten me anymore."

Pearl's jaw dropped. "When King Triton returns, I'm telling him everything!"

"You have no proof," said Ariel. "And even if he believed you, I'd tell him that I put the things back. Which is true."

Pearl was speechless. With a flurry of bubbles, she whirled around and swam off.

Just then Flounder came darting out from behind a rock. "Ariel! I saw your shells floating away," he panted. "Why did you let them go?"

"Because now I'm free of Pearl!" Ariel cried.

Flounder smiled. "Well," he said, "they're not *totally* gone." He held up one of the treasures he'd managed to save.

"Flounder!" Ariel cried as she took the last of the *see*shells. "You saved one!" She hugged her friend and placed the treasure on his head. "Come on, let's put it in the grotto before someone else sees it!"

When Ariel returned to the palace, she went straight to her room. As she passed Pearl's room, she saw her busily packing.

"You're leaving?" Ariel asked.

"My parents sent a message. They're back from vacation—and not a moment too soon, either. I've decided I don't like it here, after all." With that, Pearl stuck her nose in the air and went back to packing.

In her own bedroom, Ariel took an adventure story from the shelf. She settled in on her bed and began to read.

Around dinnertime, there was a knock on her door. "Can I come in?" asked King Triton.

Ariel floated off her bed. "Father, I want to tell you something. I'm sorry about everything that's happened. I'm not going to cause you trouble anymore."

"I've had time to think," said Triton. "It seems to me that all the trouble began when Pearl got here. I should have believed you over her in the first place. It was also wrong for me to invite her here without asking you first."

"It's okay," Ariel said.

There was a sound in the courtyard. Ariel and her father went over to the window and looked out. A coach had pulled up to the palace gate, and a parade of snails were crawling toward it, carrying Pearl's heavy suitcases on their backs.

King Triton and Ariel watched as Pearl climbed into the coach and rode away. "I have a feeling I just got my happy, carefree Ariel back," Triton said.

Ariel hugged him. "You have," she said.